SodaPop Head

Activity and Idea Book

published by

National Center for Youth Issues

Practical Guidance Resources
Educators Can Trust

ncyi.org

A special "Thanks!" to Laurel Klaassen – One of the best counselors in the business!

A Note to Parents and Educators:

Everybody gets angry. Anger is a normal human emotion. Sometimes the cause of our anger can easily be identified, other times it cannot.

When anger takes control of who we are and what we do, unfortunate things can happen. The goal of this activity book is to offer kids of all ages "hands on" tools and activities to use in controlling their anger.

It is important to teach children that it's ok to feel angry. It's what they choose to do with their anger that can make the difference. Bottling up anger or repressing it can have devastating health consequences. Letting anger out in inappropriate ways can be self-destructive.

You cannot take an angry child and "fix" him so he is no longer angry. His anger is a part of who he is. Unfortunately, if the child does not receive intervention, the anger will end up dictating who he becomes. Your best course of action is to teach the angry child how to manage his emotions and actions and channel them toward productivity…in essence, teach the child to "control his fizz!"

If we can teach children how to recognize and manage their anger, and channel it toward productive or at least acceptable outlets, they will be more successful in life.

Finally, always remember: "Laughter is the best medicine when treating the Anger Flu."

BEST!

Julia Cook

Duplication and Copyright

National Center for Youth Issues
Practical Guidance Resources
Educators Can Trust
ncyi.org

P.O. Box 22185
Chattanooga, TN 37422-2185
423.899.5714 • 800.477.8277
fax: 423.899.4547
www.ncyi.org

ISBN: 978-1-937870-02-7
© 2012 National Center for Youth Issues, Chattanooga, TN
All rights reserved.

Summary: A supplementary teacher's guide for *Soda Pop Head*.
Full of discussion questions and exercises to share with students.

Written by: Julia Cook
Contributing Editor: Laurel Klaassen
Illustrations by: Allison Valentine
Published by National Center for Youth Issues

Printed at Starkey Printing
Chattanooga, TN, USA
January 2012

The Rules for Being Angry

Directions

Have students work together to create a poster including the following rules for anger:

When I get angry:

- I will not hurt **myself**.
- I will not hurt **others**.
- I will not hurt **property**.

When the poster is completed, have each student sign the poster and promise to follow the rules. A signature is important and symbolizes a promise and a commitment.

What Makes You POP?

Materials

- Several small strips of paper
- Pen or pencil
- 2 Round balloons
- Air pump (optional)

Directions

1. Take a balloon and blow into it (or use the air pump to inflate it.) Keep blowing until it eventually pops. When it pops, talk about how it made everyone feel (i.e. scared, startled, surprised, uneasy, etc.) Explain to the group that this is how other people feel when someone around them blows up and looses their temper.

2. Have each person in the group think about the things that make them angry and have them write each thing down on a strip of paper.

3. Take turns having each person read their strips. Each time a strip is read, blow into the other balloon. (This symbolizes how anger builds up inside of us.)

4. When the balloon is very full and about to pop, let the balloon go. As it soars through the air, explain that this is what happens when we control our anger and let out our fizz. We can keep our balloon from exploding if we know what to do.

Extra!

Brainstorm as a group ways to control your fizz (let the air out of your balloon.) Suggestions may include:

- Take 5 deep breaths and clear your head.
- Walk away from the situation and find a quiet place to sit down and relax your muscles.
- Write down or draw all of your feelings on paper.
- If you are in your classroom, try sitting at your seat and do the Push Pull Dangle. (Push down hard on the seat of your chair while you count to 10. Pull up hard on the seat of your chair while you count to 10. And then dangle your arms, and feel all of your stress leave your body.)
- If you are at home, go into your room, close the door and play your music really loud.
- If you feel really angry, try punching a pillow a few times.
- Get to bed on time at night.
- Eat healthy foods.

My Anger Masterpiece

Draw a picture of what anger looks like to you.

My Human Thermometer
Watch Your Temper Temp!

Materials
- (1) 3/4" x 8" white ribbon
- (1) 3/4" x 8" red ribbon

Directions

1. Glue one end of a white 3/4" ribbon to one end of a red 3/4" ribbon.

2. Cut out the human thermometer at right. (**Note:** To make the thermometer sturdy, you may want to glue the image to posterboard or cardboard before cutting.)

3. Carefully cut slits at the top and bottom of the thermometer (use slits indicated) and run the white end of the joined ribbon through the top slits and the red end through the bottom slit. (**Note:** To make a loop, you can glue the unglued ends of the ribbon together on the backside of the thermometer. Only glue the ribbons together. Do not glue the ribbons to the thermometer.)

4. As your anger builds up, adjust your thermometer so that you will know how "hot" you are getting and when you need to find a way to lower your temper temp.

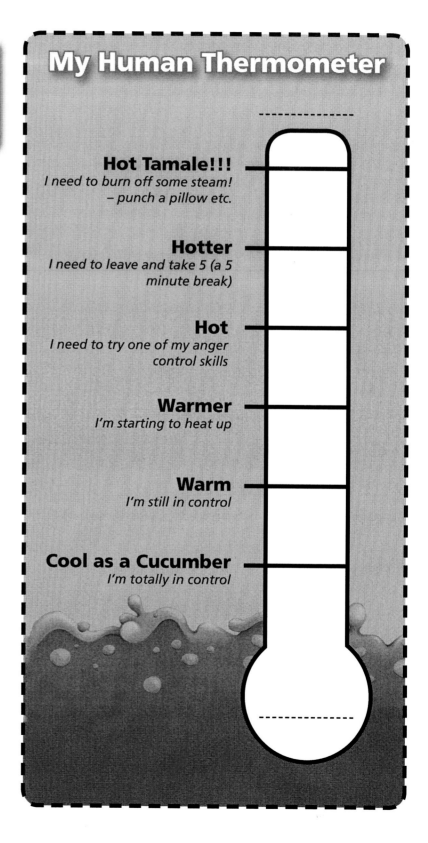

My Human Thermometer

Hot Tamale!!!
I need to burn off some steam! – punch a pillow etc.

Hotter
I need to leave and take 5 (a 5 minute break)

Hot
I need to try one of my anger control skills

Warmer
I'm starting to heat up

Warm
I'm still in control

Cool as a Cucumber
I'm totally in control

A Mental Vacation

Directions

Sometimes, when we feel stressed, we need to escape reality for a little while by going on a "mental vacation". Close your eyes and think of a calm, happy place that you would like to go. Now, make a list of as many calm, happy places that you can think of in the space below (i.e. sitting by the ocean, sitting under a tree at a park, fishing in a pond, etc.)

_____   _____

_____   _____

_____   _____

_____   _____

_____   _____

_____   _____

_____   _____

Draw a picture of your favorite calm, happy place.

Now, whenever you need to go on a "mental vacation", close your eyes and see yourself in your favorite calm, happy place. Just don't forget to come back!

My Happy Place Diorama

Make a diorama (3-D model) of your happy place. Make it as realistic as you can. Display your diorama in your classroom so that when you need to take a "mental vacation", you can look over and see where you will go!

The Cooling Cube

Materials
- 1 ice cube
- Small ziplock plastic bag

Sometimes, when you start to feel angry, your body temperature will feel like it is rising. Try using a "Cooling Cube" to keep you cool! When you first start feeling hot, put an ice cube in a ziplock bag and close it tight. Hold the ice cube in your hand and feel its coolness against your skin. As the ice cube melts, imagine your anger peacefully melting away with it.

My Frustration Plan

I know when I am starting to get angry because my:

_____

_____

The first thing I should do when this happens is to:

_____

_____

If that doesn't work, I should try to:

_____

_____

If I feel like I need to leave the room so that I won't blow my bottle cap,
I need to give my teacher the signal that looks like this:

_____

_____

My plan to release my fizz once I have left my classroom is to:

_____

_____

When I feel like I am in control of my fizz again, I should walk back into
my classroom and get back on task as soon as I can. When I come in,
my teacher will know that I feel more in control.

I promise that I will not abuse this privilege in any way.

_____
Student's Signature

_____
Teacher's Signature

_____
Counselor's Signature

9

Time To Color

Sock it to 'EM!

Materials

- Clean crew or dress socks (laundry orphans work great for this one!)
- Several small strips of paper
- Pen or pencil

Directions

Think of everything that makes you angry and write each one on a strip of paper. Place the strips inside the sock. Tie a knot in the sock so the strips of paper cannot come out. Now, the next time you get angry, take your sock and throw it against the wall, stomp on it, squeeze it, stretch it, etc. Do whatever it takes to "sock it to your anger!"

Bubble Wrap Blast!!!

The next time you feel angry, take a piece of bubble wrap and "POP" your anger away. Every time you hear a pop, take a breath. You just "popped" a small part of what is making you angry, and now that part is gone!

For small reasons, just a pop or two will do it. If you have a big reason for being angry, try twisting the bubble wrap, or even stomping on it!!!

Be in control of your anger and…POP it away!

Homemade Soda POP! – Just for Fun!

Root Beer Soda

The Frugal Gourmet Whole Family Cookbook

Time: 10 minutes
Serves: 8

Ingredients

2 cups sugar
1 cup water
1 tablespoon root beer extract
64 ounces carbonated water

Instructions

1. Stir 2 cups sugar into 1 cup of water and just heat until all dissolves and is clear.

2. Add 1 tablespoon of root beer extract to complete syrup.

3. Place 2 ounces of syrup in a 12 oz. soda glass.

4. Add a little ice and soda to fill: 8 ounces of soda to 2 ounces of syrup. Stir only once so that you don't work out the carbonation.

It will keep you COOL!

The Old Fashioned Method
(by Ctraugh – www.foods.com)

Ingredients:
- 1 gallon water
- 2 cups water (for making extract)
- 2 ounces fresh ginger root
- 2 cups sugar
- 1 tablespoon vanilla extract
- 1/8 teaspoon yeast

Directions:
1. Slice the ginger into thin sections and add them to two cups of boiling water.
2. Simmer this on very low heat for 20 minutes.
3. While this is simmering, boil one gallon of water and two cups of sugar for one minute and set aside.
4. Pour the ginger and liquid into a blender and blend on high for about one minute.
5. Pour this blend into the sugar water, through a strainer.
6. With a soup ladle, pour a few cups of the hot brew through the remaining pulp to extract a bit more of the ginger flavor.
7. Cool to room temperature. When cool, add vanilla, yeast and stir until dissolved.
8. Let sit for about 30 minutes.
9. Then bottle and age.
10. The simplest, safest and least expensive method of bottling is to use one-liter plastic soft drink bottles with screw caps.
11. These can be sterilized by rinsing in a mixture of household bleach and water and then rinsed with clean water.
12. After filling, the bottles should be set aside at room temperature for about 48 hours, or until hard (check by squeezing).
13. Then refrigerate to finish the aging process.
14. Leaving the bottles at room temperature too long will cause over carbonation.
15. Using glass rather than plastic bottles can cause shattered bottles.
16. Another nice feature of the plastic bottles is that they can be re-carbonated if only partially consumed.
17. Just let it sit out over night with the cap on and refrigerate it when hard.

POP Your Anger Away!

Blow bubbles from the bottle and have kids pop them as fast as they can. Each time they pop a bubble, explain that they have just popped away something that has made them angry.

Stress Dough

Using the recipe below, work together with your child to create his very own stress dough.

Stress dough is great for squeezing, pulling, stretching and smashing out your anger. Keep some on hand so that when you need it, it can help you let out your fizz!

Extra-rubbery stress dough recipe

(playdoughrecipe.com)
- 1 and a half cups of colored water
- 1 cup of cornstarch
- 2 cups of baking soda

Preparation:
Mix all ingredients together and boil over medium heat. Once doughy, remove from heat. Knead, shape and mold. Store in a refrigerated, sealed container.

You or Your Anger... Who's the Boss?

Sometimes, when you let your anger be the boss of you, you lose control.

Draw a picture of what that looks like:

How does losing control make you feel?

_____

_____

When you lose control, how does that make other people around you feel?

_____

_____

You or Your Anger...
Who's the Boss, Two?

When you become the boss of your anger, you are in control.

Draw a picture of what that looks like:

How does being the boss of your anger make you feel?

_____

_____

How do other people around you feel when you are in control of your anger?

_____

_____

Make Your Own Soda POP Head

Materials

- 1 empty plastic soda pop bottle
- A cork that will fit snugly in the end of the bottle
- 2 tablespoons of baking soda
- 1 square of toilet paper
- 1 cup of vinegar

Directions:

1. Fit the cork tightly into the opening of the soda pop bottle. If it is too loose, you can wrap tape around the cork to make it fit better.

2. Make a fuel packet. Place two tablespoons of baking soda into the middle of a square of toilet paper. Fold the square up tightly so that it doesn't come apart easily and so that baking soda does not leak out. Also make sure the packet will fit easily through the bottle's opening.

3. Put on safety glasses and pour one cup of vinegar into the bottle.

4. Drop in a packet of baking soda and quickly seal the opening with the cork.

5. Immediately put the bottle on the ground pointing the cork up and back away. In a few seconds the toilet paper will dissolve in the vinegar. As the baking soda and vinegar mix, this will create carbon dioxide gas, building up pressure in the bottle. When the pressure is sufficient, the cork will pop out of the bottle, just like when your anger builds up inside of you.

6. What does it feel like anticipating when the cork will blow?

7. When the cork does blow out, how does it make you feel?

8. How do you think other kids feel when you blow your bottle cap?

Warnings

- Always do this project outside. The bottle may travel quite far and the cork will pop out with a great deal of force. In addition, it will leave a trail of foam spewing out the bottle.
- Always wear your safety glasses to prevent any injury from the cork or foam spewing out.

Reference: http://www.ehow.com/how_6498045_make-car-baking-soda-vinegar.html#ixzz1eHPPRCBu

Frustration Bread

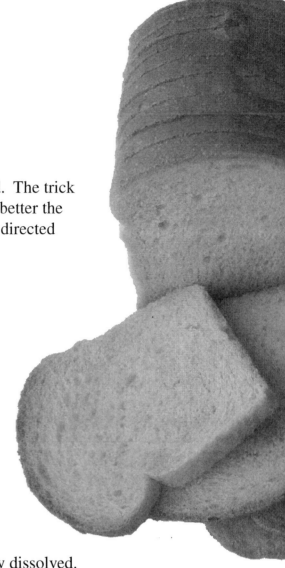

Using the recipe below, work together to create Frustration Bread. The trick to making great bread is the kneading! The more you knead, the better the bread…and the less angry you feel! Prepare Frustration Bread as directed and ENJOY a nice, tasty, anger-free treat!

Ingredients
- 1 package dry yeast
- ¼ cup warm water
- ½ cup milk
- ¼ cup sugar
- 1 teaspoon salt
- 3 tablespoons softened margarine
- 2 ¾ cups flour
- 1 egg
- 1 heavy duty gallon sized ziplock bag per recipe

Directions
1. Dissolve yeast in warm water inside of ziplock bag.
2. Seal the bag and using hands to mix, make sure yeast is fully dissolved.
3. Add milk, sugar, salt and margarine to bag.
4. Add in about 1 cup of flour to make a batter.
5. Mix by kneading outside of bag.
6. Add egg and mix by squeezing the bag for one minute.
7. Stir in 1 more cup of flour and knead to form a soft dough.
8. KNEAD! KNEAD!! KNEAD all of your anger away!!! Or until dough is smooth and elastic (adding flour if necessary).
9. Take ziplock bag home, and knead once more.
10. Remove from bag, shape into bread pan, and allow to raise to twice the original size (about an hour)
11. Bake at 375 degrees until golden brown. While bread is rising in the pan, talk to your parents about how you were able to knead your anger away!

Enjoy sharing your bread with your family.

Note: If this activity is done in the morning at school, store ziplock bags in refrigerator to prevent Frustration Bread from over-rising.

You Be the Soda POP Head Expert

Your teacher informs you that a younger student in your building is struggling with anger. He blows his cap at least 3 times a day. The other kids are afraid to play with him because he gets so angry. The teachers don't know how to help him, but since you are now in control of your cap, they feel that you might know what to do. Your job is to teach him to become a Soda Pop Head Anger Expert who can control his bottle cap.

Using the space below, write out a plan for this young Soda Pop Head and explain how you can help him.

First, I would…

_____

_____

_____

Next, I would…

_____

_____

_____

Then, I would…

_____

_____

_____

Finally, I would…

_____

_____

_____

How would you be able to tell if your plan was working?

_____

_____

_____

The Anger Collage

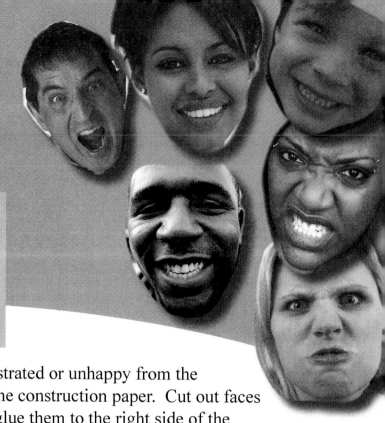

Materials
- (1) 12" x 18" piece of construction paper folded in half
- Magazines
- Glue stick

Cut out faces of people who look angry, frustrated or unhappy from the magazines and glue then to the left side of the construction paper. Cut out faces of people who look happy and content and glue them to the right side of the construction paper. Compare each side of your collage with the other.

How does it make you feel when you look at the left side of the paper?

_____

_____

_____

How does it make you feel when you look at the right side of the paper?

_____

_____

_____

Which side would people who know you best place your face? Why?

_____

_____

_____

Was it easier for you to find pictures for the right side or the left side? Why?

_____

_____

_____

How Short is Your Fuse?

Sometimes, we have days when our fuse seems to be shorter than others. In other words, our patience is short and we are angered easily. It's always best to have a long fuse. You need to be aware when you are having a "short fuse" day…and alert others as well.

Figure One

Figure Two

Figure Three

1. Cut out the "Fuse Monitor" label below. Glue it to the toilet paper tube as shown. (Figure One)

2. Tie a paper clip to one end of the string. Put a small hole in the center of the cloth and thread the non-paper clip end of the string through the hole. Tie a knot in the string so it does not go back through the hole. (Figure Two)

3. Secure the cloth to the tube as shown and clip the end of the string to the other edge of the tube. Adjust your fuse as needed. (Figure Three)

Keep your "Fuse Monitor" near by and remember to adjust your fuse according to the way you are feeling. This can be a great way to monitor your anger and let you know when you need to let out your *"FIZZ!"*

FUSE MONITOR

Extra! Extra! Extra! There are special people in our lives that are our "Fuse Lengtheners". They help us figure out ways to make our fuses longer so we don't blow up. Make a list of your "Fuse Lengtheners" on a separate sheet of paper.

The Human Barometer

Directions:
- On a separate sheet of paper, make a list of every feeling you have ever felt (i.e. angry, happy, sad, hopeless, etc.) If your feelings were weather, what would they look like?
- Using the worksheet below, write down the feelings from your list under the weather category that matches them best. (i.e. sunny = happy, peaceful, content. Tornado = angry and out of control, etc.)

Sunny	Partly Cloudy	Light Rain
Thunder Storm	Tornado	Snowy

Answer the following questions:

1. How do you know when the weather is going to get bad?

_____

2. What do you do to prepare for bad weather?

_____

3. How do you know when you are starting to get angry? (What does it feel like?)

_____

4. What can you do to prepare yourself when you start to feel angry?

_____

It Takes One to Know One!

Interview a person that you know who is a soda pop head (at least sometimes)
and ask him/her the following questions:

1. Think of a time in your life when you were young and you lost your temper. What happened?

2. How did this experience affect your life?

3. Did you have consequences for losing your temper?

4. If the same thing had happened today, what would you have done differently?

5. Looking back, what advice do you have that will help me control my temper?

Will It Matter?

Sometimes we end up making a bigger deal out of things that happen to us than we need to. This activity can help you keep things in perspective.

Directions:

Think of something that has recently made you very angry. On a separate sheet of paper, answer the following questions.

What happened?

Now, ask yourself honestly, will what happened to you matter in:

- 5 minutes from now? (If so, why?)
- 5 hours from now? (If so, why?)
- 5 days from now? (If so, why?)
- 5 weeks from now? (If so, why?)
- 5 months from now? (If so, why?)
- 5 years from now? (If so, why?)

Looking back, should you have gotten so angry? Why or why not?

I Need to Take Five!

Materials Needed
- (1) empty 20 oz. soda or water bottle
- Permanent markers

Directions

Cut out the "Take Five" label and color it with the markers. Paste it on the 20 oz. bottle. (You may want to make your own special label).

How to Use

There are times when a student just has to step away from a situation for a few minutes to keep from blowing his/her bottle cap. Usually, this can be done in about five minutes.

Brainstorm with your students, places they can go before they blow:
- Counselor's office
- Walk down the hallway and back
- Go to the library
- Go get a drink
- Walk to the office
- Go to the gym and work off some steam
- Etc.

Establish as a group a plan to "Take Five" in advance. Make sure your staff is aware of your "Take Five" plan as well. Use "Fuse Lengtheners" to help you whenever possible (see bottom of page 21). Then, when a student needs to leave for a few minutes, have them grab the "Take Five" bottle and make visual contact with you so that you know what they are doing. Over-emphasize that the "Take Five" bottle will not be needed by everyone, is a privilege, and is not to be taken advantage of.

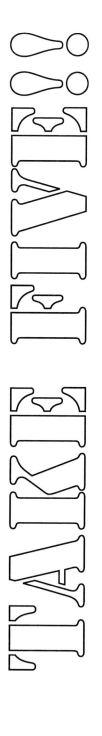

TAKE FIVE!